PRIMAL DOMINATION

Drexicon Breeding Auction

Sci-Fi Alien Romance

Book One

Snow Morningstar

TABLE OF CONTENTS

EPIGRAPH:

"I dawdle deep in your spots, as your spots are my happy lascivious thoughts"

PROLOGUE

When Earth becomes barren, wars are waged between two species.

Humans and the Drexicons.

No one remembers when the Drexicons came, or why they did.

The only thing humans know is they never left.

The last of the humans are driven to survive on a boat known as the beacon.

The Earth is barren, along with the Drexicon females.

A prophecy is told. It will save the humans and Drexicons, uniting them as one.

One human female and one Drexicon male will bore a child to save them all.

One magic child.

The humans agreed to auction off their fertile females, in exchange for compensation.

Thump thump thump......

The sounds of boots hit hard on the land of Drexicons, the earth rumbles and trembles when everyone keeps running and moving at a great pace. The big aliens running with two tiny horns decorated as an ornament on either side of their head and their bodies marching in unison towards the giant golden temple. A temple they visit on

Tuesdays for meditation and linking their brain's eye to a realm above the universe and rotating messages alongside their vision and memory. But today was different and the place of peace would attempt to open their minds to a solution they desperately desired.

"March fast chief," says a Drexicon from beneath his breath.

"We must take two steps in a half-second now," says the chief, quickly calculating his steps in the mind.

"Noted sir," says the Army of alien male warriors jiggling their legs; and their big bulge was always visible from beneath their pants, showing their huge male organs.

The Drexicon alien-men didn't find any females to mate with for a long time. And they had no choice but to stick their thick heavy organs in other men; because their alien females were too small in their space for them, with no elasticity in their female organs and abnormality in their brains. In the worst cases of desperation, Epsilon heard of men using animals.

"Why don't we cut our females to make more room for our dicks?" Suggested a protector in the meeting within the temple, while discussing important breeding concerns.

"Cutting them won't fix the issue because they have no elasticity in their vaginas like human females," concluded a specialist in the team, "they don't possess the same elasticity in their asshole or cunt to hold a cock, which is the same with every Drexicon female in this generation now for two decades." With that conclusion, the meeting was called to a close.

Epsilon never mated with a Drexicon female, male or animal. All he got were the wet dreams and an aching hard cock, always making him restless in long alone nights...

Meditation and connection remained a strong practice and only the most dedicated, ruthless, and powerful chiefs could exercise it religiously making their dreams stay connected with the future. Epsilon Kristos (The chief and the alluring Drexicon possessing the high intelligentsia and power struck looks) leads the first row, marching his feet on the barren soil, and competing for his pace......mindlessly. Silently.

The noise of their boots hammering the ground sent jolts and sensationalizing waves through the heart of the earth; while the heat melts the delicate skin on the forehead of Drexicons, making their horns stiff and brown from the scorching sun. Little beads of sweat appear in a disarray of patterns on their foreheads. And their well-built muscular bodies push each step rhythmically to reach the pinnacle of success. Everyone patiently waited for this day when the moon was to be full and bright in the sky and, no signs of the sun in sight with no stars to accompany the moon as well. Infertility and humans have marred Drexicons for long and now they needed a solution.

The Drexicons and humans stand at the opposite ends of defeat from each other. They didn't realize that while fighting with each other they were calling death and wrath on themselves. But no one was winning at this battle of blood. Humans were eating each other, skating with pangs of hunger on their last dying days on the beacon (the last human settlement on a dilapidated boat)......and practicing cannibalism, eating the meat of their brothers for survival...

The night was about to fall any minute dissipating the heat, and embracing the dark clouds. And the nameless sound of prophecy would ring in the temple as a last resort to save a life. The last resort and savior in times of turmoil. The never-ending wars with humans had broken the backs of fierce Drexicons. They had to reach the beacon before the next dawn and listen to the golden words of fulfillment. The anticipation grew and each mind was racing to find their way to be the next Drexicon Chief. It was easy and simple. And open for all.

The opportunity held their breath and clutched their hearts right pinning through their chest. The most powerful Drexicon of all times could be born salvaging life, slaving all humans, aliens, and animals with his enormous magically unbounded powers.

The dream was knocking on their doors to be manifested into an astounding reality...

"Hey come back," says Epsilon from behind, running at full speed trying to catch her. She always shows him a glimpse of herself and then vanishes in the dark somewhere. Epsilon kept trying to find her, like a mad alien in the joys of seeking some comfort in holding her and sniffing her hairs. Her beautiful fragrance hits his nostrils and he runs after her...sniffing like a hungry dog...

She was different than anyone he ever saw around him. And the white pure light emancipating from her body always gave him immense calm like he was floating in the air and his whole existence becoming light. But he lost her each time. And he tries to find her like a mad warrior in his dreams. Battling to find her, the beautiful female. His swords become useless all of a sudden and he feels like she cuts him in his chest without any weapon...

"Come Back," shouts Epsilon...

"I want you," he screams with terror and tears...

"Please I beg you...." he continues...

"Ahhhhrghhhhh," screams Epsilon, from out of his night terror fully drenched in sweat. His nightmares felt so calm when he would be experiencing them in their subconscious realm but as soon as he opened his eyelids from the beep of his ancient watch, he would find his erection making a tent in his soft blanket and his horns felt hot to the touch.

The saltish sweat poured over his horns like some melted ice, romancing his hot horns and he would come back to senses not knowing what to do, running out of his tent like a child gasping for fresh cool air. Nobody knew that The Chief, with all his exotic charms, had night terrors and a female that followed him in his dreams making him run and follow her......

"What do those dreams had to do with my life?" Epsilon always asked himself. No one could solve the conundrum for him. The same face and same feelings. Nothing changed about her face and her features fully etched on his memory. His wild feelings for her remained a puzzle for Epsilon to solve...

Does she even exist? His wonderings would trouble him all day while he would focus his arrow at the flesh of the nicely shaped buck.

From the golden temple, a voice rang through the air.

'And the prophecy entails a young fertile woman and a strong alien man mating and consuming each other in mating, flesh, and desire and making this miracle child be born as the savior of the planets...a small introduction before the final verdict on rules...'

The voice echoed in between the little chirps of the crickets......It was a heavy staunch accent with an air of control and dominance, and everything fell completely silent in the round golden temple. And even the animals stayed still lending their ears to the strange voice...

The humans and the Drexicons are the last Illuminati with a strengthened nervous system upheld high on their necks, and hard dense bones to show prowess over alien, uncultured elements. They inhibit the planet green right in this time and their extinction is mandatory...

If the child and protector of the Drexicon throne aren't born out of the blood of an alien male and womb of a human female, with the mother specie bearing a male child and a scar on her inner thigh, and the couple copulating and ejaculating in no less than 600 seconds.

Their convulsions must be timed together to materialize the prophecy of a magic child.......

The silence prevails while everyone tries to make the meaning out of the words just punched hard at them and think deep in their brains on how to possess this child in their homes. The same did cross the mind of humans hiding behind the thick bushes overhearing the prophecy. The game to rule just begins......

CHAPTER 1
THE HUMAN GIRLS GET TRAINED TO SEDUCE ALIEN MEN BY AUNT LEXICON

"You act like a woman but you are our soldiers"

For as long as we can remember, the Drexicons want to defeat humans and kill them," says the old woman with a deep sigh deeper than the wrinkles on her forehead.

The boat was stagnant in the water and the handful of humans dreaded death every day from the aliens. They had no arrows or weapons anymore and now they were starting to shrink in population.

"Did you hear the prophecy," asks the younger woman with utter suspicion.

"Yes, God has his plans now," sighs the old lady and tries to find a ray of hope in the dark gloomy sky.

"Humans' survival becomes important to breed the next generation of the Drexicons," the younger woman says while trying to charge the solar batteries in the sun. The army stood alert on the base to fight any aliens, but they had to use their brains now, because they were weaponless.

"Yes, they are in abundance and their brains work faster than humans," says the old woman now looking at the dead batteries.

The humans (rich with fertile women) also grapple with

extinction because of being limited to that ancient boat running on batteries. They needed batteries, power cells, and gold to survive on their ship, and barter for food. All of which was in possession of Drexicons in exchange for their vivacious virgins to give birth to the next Drexicon generations. The prophecy held a possibility for them both and now they had to groom their girls to be ready for the Drexicon males.

"All the girls between thirteen to nineteen must line up in the queue early in the morning, they will be evaluated and they must have started menstruating," says the announcement from the speaker of the boat when Moon and Leila were chewing the dry bread they found in the pantry. It was a time when everyone on the boat was rushing to sleep after the long tiring day at work. The battle to survive each day.

"What is it all about?" asks Leila in disbelief who just turned eighteen, but looks smaller and malnourished than her age.

God had been extra careful and generous when creating Moon. He carved her body like a live painting of an artist with shapely, large breasts and dark brown areolas with stiff nipples which elongate when she would quiver or when her body would feel aroused. Any man could fit his lips on her nipples and suck them for hours holding her breasts firmly in his hands. At seventeen, she already looked like a fully developed woman of a man's dreams but her mother always kept her safe from prying eyes. Her tiny waist held the weight of her big breasts and her booty would jiggle when she walked.

"This sounds scary," says Moon while licking her fingers.

"The command is from Aunt Lexicon," says Leila suspiciously while eating a morsel of bread in her mouth.

"Are they getting us married?" Moon asks, while a frightening light flickers through her eyes.

In this enclosed ship her dreams of dancing and singing were already laid to rest and she opened her eyes to the terrors of alien shooters shooting arrows or swords at them. Though she bore a sweet spot for aliens because they always followed the rules. Humans never did that.

The humans were always conspiring and never even stayed back from eating their brothers. Moon felt disgusted by everyone now with lost dreams always returning to her eyes on lonely nights. The idea disgusted her and she left her bread unfinished. She saw a man eating his wife one night on the boat and she vomited the whole night that day swearing in her heart to never marry a human. The only thing she desired was to marry an alien-man with strong principles. A powerful alien-man would offer her protection, and a welcomed reprieve from the beacon.

Moon fantasized about dancing in his arms and singing lullabies for him. The idea made her heart warm and her dreams powerful to keep her moving each day from the monotony of life, and the evil deeds of the other humans.

"Moon, we should sleep so we can wake up early to get in line before they thrash us with sticks," says Leila while sticking her body deep inside the torn blanket.

"Come inside and make me warm," asks Leila with a sheepish grin.

Moon slides in with Leila and they both press against each other to generate some warmth in their flimsy blanket, trying to shut their eyes and not think about the next day and what conundrums it might hold for them.

All the girls stood straight in the queue waiting for the orders to come when they saw Aunt Lexicon appearing on the deck. In her mid-forties, she looked younger than her age with a red shirt showing all her braless boobs and tight pants sticking to her legs. Her hair was all loose and red from some tint and had freckles on her nose making her look sun-tanned.

She took good care of herself, despite the circumstances. She kept herself alive on board by seducing men and taking favors from them while giving them a decent fuck here and there. And everyone heard strange rumors about her engaging in bad activities at night but she was the most experienced person who could train these girls to be ready for the alien-men. Her experience couldn't be negated and the matter engaged life and death for humans.

"There came a prophecy from the lands of the golden temple," says Lexicon while clearing her throat. The girls stand straight trying to twiddle their fingers and grasp the meaning of a prophecy. For they only knew hunger, arrows, batteries, and death...though seeing a lady clad in red and speaking to them was a welcome sight for them.

"A prophecy was foretold at the golden temple. And the prophecy claimed a Drexicon man and a human female rescuing the endangered lands and blowing the seeds of fertility in the barren soil because Drexicon females cannot bear children. It is said that a human female and a Drexicon male will produce a magic child. The born magic child will rule the world of Drexicons and humans with enormous powers. The power to resurrect the dead, the chance to travel through time, and a brain so intelligent that it can equal one million humans," Aunt Lexicon explained.

The prophecy held hope for Drexicons and humans. The Drexicons would get females, and humans would get batteries and money in exchange. The money through auction was needed by humans to chance their way through this magic child.

"We need to snatch the magic child from the aliens and resurrect our dead loved ones," says Aunt Lexicon in a long hard speech while a small tear swam in her eye thinking about her lost family.

"But how can we contribute to this mission," asks a girl with utter naivety and innocence not being able to grasp the concept of their mission.

"You just need to spread your poor little pussy and make the Drexicon men mad for you," replied Aunt Lexicon with a tone full of spite.

She couldn't believe that these girls didn't even know a thing about sex and she had to work like an animal to train them because with their current state they would only shoo the men away.

"We will hold an auction where you will all be nicely dressed and presented to the aliens and if they like you then, they will bid for you and you will become their bride," says Lexicon, "But once you become their bride you need to make sure to get pregnant with the child and then flee back to the human camp, the child will be ours," she adds while keeping her tone low so no one can hear her at all. The soldiers elaborated to her that she needed to perform this job perfectly and she will get her due right.

The girls feel hopeful that they may get something more now. They had heard stories about Drexicons eating roasted meats and singing songs around a bonfire. They have heard only fables about such good times. A chance at life offered by God to them now.

"I will do a detailed inspection of your bodies and then your training will begin," says Lexicon in a dry cracky voice.

She goes inside in a private room and calls the first girl.

"Strip," she says while looking at her from beyond her glasses analyzing every inch of her existence.

The timid girl takes off all her clothes in a little of a second, leaving nothing behind for Lexicon's imagination.

She stands from her chair and roughly rubs her hands on the girl's chest which was almost flat with no depth.

"You feel something," she asks.

"No, umm, noo madam," the girl barely speaks.

"Put one finger in your sex," she commands.

The girl opens her legs trying to locate her hole to put a finger in.

"Okay stop," says Lexicon and orders her to leave.

These girls didn't know much about sexuality and she needed to train them enough to stand in front of deadly aliens and win a battle for humans.

The girls keep coming and none of them impresses Lexicon enough. They had to be severely groomed with limited resources and needed to be schooled to have a great impact on the Drexicons.

"Next," says Aunt Lexicon busily while stifling a yawn and gazing out at the calm sea. They had been floating in water for years never really finding a way to reach the land but now the hope shone with a chance of wealth coming and they could get the miracle child too with some proper planning. The only information and supplies they received were from Drexicon messengers. The beacon didn't have enough power to start the engines. The batteries they had were merely enough to turn the lights on at night.

Lexicon was deep in her reverie when she heard Moon saying, "Lady Lexicon, I am here."

She didn't realize how much time passed since she was standing there and when she looked at her, she got startled for a moment and her jaw dropped open in disbelief.

Those long dark coffee eyes with full curled eyelashes and thick brows, flushed cheekbones, and strong jaw with a mole near her lips. Her hair was tied at the nape with a few naughty strands caressing her face.

"If she could take Lexicon's breath away, then what effect could she have on men?" says Lexicon out loud, while coming a little nearer to her.

Lexicon never saw this girl before or maybe she was guarded by her mother in some nook. But whatever the case might be she was undoubtedly a beauty beyond heavens.

So sexy and seductive with innocence plastered all over her face. The girl was oblivious to her beauty.

"Strip," she commands.

Moon hesitates for a minute as she was a virgin and no one ever saw her naked. She started bleeding last month and now she had to get naked in front of this woman.

She didn't have a choice and she slowly started undoing her top button while trying not to look into Lexicons' prying gaze. Her shirt was open with her boobs ready to spring out when she bent down to take off her trousers and Lexicon couldn't help but gasp at the hungry view of her breasts hanging down. She abruptly took off her trousers and to Lexicon's delight, she had no bra on. It was a complete show anyone could enjoy watching and her innocence mixed with her sexiness was quite an intoxicating cocktail and a heady mix to handle. Her finger undoing the last buttons while standing erect now and the sweet white swell of her breasts peeking from beneath. This girl needed some real-time lovemaking by a strong man. She was perfect.

"Fast," orders Lexicon while trying to look stern but she could hardly get hold of her excitement to see this goddess in her full glory. Lexicon herself feels a little wet in her panties though she never doubted herself to be a lesbian and badly wanted to rub her clitoris on this magical beauty.

Moon stood all naked and exotic in front of Lexicon while looking at the ground not knowing what to do.

"Turn around," she orders, and Moon mechanically turns around quickly exposing her round sexy ass and her long hair falling till the back of her body just above her ass-cheek. She absent-mindedly places one hand on her ass, making the back view all the more appealing.

The girl didn't need any grooming or improvement. In her present form, she had the power to win dynasties just by spreading her long beautiful legs in front of a man and could melt him there and then.

"Finger yourself with wide legs," says Lexicon, and Moon feels shocked with color growing deep on her beautiful cheeks but she couldn't dare resist and with utmost courage rub her finger on her plump vagina. Untouched and never fingered.

"Let me show it to you, baby," says Lexicon coquettishly, while pinching her clitoris in her two fingers and Moon shrieked with pain.

"I will teach you how to make a man weak in his knees and how to moan in front of him," says Lexicon cunningly while gently massaging her clitoris and pressing her soft gooey boobs with her other hand. Moon observed Lexicon with rapt attention.

Lexicon needed to keep this girls' virginity intact as she was their golden hen.

Moon felt so weak and shy but she liked what Lexicon was doing to her...Ummm....her private parts.

Moon saw some hope to be with a man and leave this stinky boat.....and she had to learn a lot from Lexicon on how to please a man in bed. And to pleasure herself. Living one day from the next in a battle for survival, Moon had never thought much about pleasure.

Though Moon pledged in her heart to never return to the beacon. Lexicon couldn't guess her motives while she was completely lost in her soft sexy vagina.

"Dress up girl you have a lot to learn," says Lexicon while studying her notes and coming back to her senses. She can't get lost in the beauty of a chick completely forgetting her goals to earn extra batteries. She has some plans, to live a great life after all.

"Will my dream of marrying an alien man come true?" Moon says, while picking up her shirt from the floor. Maybe the guiding angels were on her side after all......she thought while buttoning her shirt and hiding properly before that big day...

The training started the next day and all the girls were summoned right after the dawn peeked in the sky. Lexicon commands them to bring sticks and a piece of wood. They were lined up and all were given a strange box neatly wrapped in a shiny wrapper.

"Hello Girls," says Lexicon standing on the podium and looking down at them like a big shark ready to feed on their bones like prey.

"Hello Lady," echoed the girls in unison, like some untouched slaves ready in turn to be slaughtered.

"We are at a war and it's been long even before you were born. But this time the war is not to kill with weapons but to kill with your looks and win this war without killing a single alien," she says like a professor of philosophy trying hard to put some brain in her peers.

"Your weapon lays right and tight in between your legs and you must know that Drexicons haven't mated with females in more than two decades. Because of the strange abnormality in the holes of their women, and most are either masturbating or using animals for their fuck," says Lexicon and looking rigidly in the eyes of each girl.

Her gaze could absorb information better in their brains than her words alone.

"Now they are not only women hungry, but children hungry. They are dying out, the same as us. And after a great hallmark a ceasefire has been decided between humans and aliens and a consensus is reached to auction our virgin girls," says Lexicon. She takes a bite of an apple, holding in her hand to quickly wet her parched throat. The soldier just smuggled it to her early in the morning while she was making her notes and he was fucking her ass from behind. The hot memory makes her sweat and she clears her throat to bring her attention back to the present.

"I briefly explained it to you in person. But now is the time to train you as we have just ten days before the auction and we want to sell as many girls as possible, so not only do you have a great future as a Drexicon Bride but a chance to be a mother of the miracle child and help your human race back to life," says Lexicon while taking the last bite of her forbidden fruit.

The girls stood still like statues and listened to her and most of what she said. It made sense because they all wanted a luxurious life as the wife of a Drexicon.

They were famous for their gallant wars, courage and they led a great life full of fruits and soirees served on their tables with great advancement in science and intelligent brains unlike this drowning beacon of humans. Which was not only drowning itself, but drowning their precious fate as well.

"Carefully look at the soap, rose petals, and shampoo to clean your bodies and rub these petals early in the morning and wear clean clothes, and use the thread to floss your teeth," explains Lexicon while squarely looking at Moon, who was shining like the morning sun in the cool breeze.

Lexicon would love eating Moon's pussy herself, if the charged batteries weren't involved. She dreamt of buying gold and a ferry and traveling the world with a sexy man of her own.

"Now all of you strip naked and hold this book on your head. Hold this stick on the blades of your shoulders and walk. Make sure none of it falls off," says Lexicon, "you need to walk like a swan while shaking your bosom and booties, to get those Drexicons' to drool all over you," adds Lexicon.

The girls do as commanded and after a long day of practice on empty stomachs, they manage to learn to walk with a little sway in their legs and the right amount of jiggle in their boobs and asses. They were served a proper dinner with instructions to groom before early dawn the next day.

"You have the meatiest boobs in the whole lot," says Leila talking to Moon at night, "All the girls were staring at you when you were walking," she says trying not to think about herself.

"Don't worry Leila, Aunt Lexicon will teach you to massage with herbs to increase your size," says Moon with a hint of sympathy in her eyes.

She knew that Leila was too average looking for a man to bid on her but with proper care, she could groom herself.

"It's very embarrassing to get rejected Moon. And what will I do here alone after you are gone?" Asks Leila, in a bleak tone.

"No one knows the fate as of yet, Leila. Maybe it's you who goes and I don't get selected," says Moon.

Moon and Leila slept together, hand in hand thinking about a future they didn't know. But everything felt so strange that they stopped thinking about anything a long time ago. Aboard the beacon, the next day was never a guarantee. Aunt Lexicon would teach them to groom themselves and moan with pleasure. Fingering and orgasm, and different sex positions. But who knew what could happen to them?

Moon looked at Leila who was sound asleep and quietly slipped her hand in her shirt finding the place she never explored before. She saw the girls Oooohing and aaahing looking at her and she felt the hot gazes fixated on her body all the long. She never saw herself in the light that people saw her and now slowly rolling her hand up the felt stomach she finds a little depth and then a big mountain-like curve taking her to her finely shaped hard nipple. She cups her boob in her hand and gently pats it while the shirt rubs against her already erect nipple, making her squeeze her moan in her throat.

Moon grabs her one full left boob in her hand and now travels her right hand in her pajamas where she finds a beautiful line hiding her ultimate prize. She lovingly holds her full vagina, cupped in her hand. Then parts the lips joined together with her finger sliding it deep, in her so wet valley. Leila moves and Moon stills her both hands and closes her eyes. After a while, she hears her snoring and this time moves a little further from Leila to continue on her journey to self-explore.

Her own body made throbbing a heat pulse between her thighs. And she opened her legs a little to explore her wetness more. Moon rubs herself the way Aunt lexicon did and she felt a strange thing, a sensation, build in her tummy. Like a ball of pleasure rolling and becoming big with her every stroke of her clit.

With her other hand, she grabs her breasts in her hand and brings it close to her mouth to lick her elongated nipple and suck on it like a small child. Moon didn't take long to orgasm and delve deep into pieces exploding all around her body while pushing her ass frantically in her palm.

Moon's orgasm makes her sleep instantly with one hand fully placed on her plump pussy and her breasts in the other. It was a tiring day of learning, unlearning, and unwinding and a day to know that she could flatter anyone existent on earth including herself. A knowledge so precious for her existentialism.

CHAPTER 2
VIRGIN AND SCAR

"My shining moon with a rigid scar"

It was the big day. It was the day of the auction. The men from Drexicon marched into the large beacon holding humans, the last left on Earth and only hope for the extinguishing Drexicons. The thoughts clouded Epsilon's mind and he was not paying much attention towards the chanting of voices ringing around him. Epsilon casually scanned the room and he was feeling suffocated with all the humans clamored up in this tiny space.

"Check the batteries in the bag," he commanded to his protector.

"Roger Sir," Protector says with a little bow in his head. Using a small hand-held device, the protector scanned all of Epsilon's batteries, making sure they were fully charged.

Epsilon stands still patiently waiting for him to respond.

"Batteries all charged and intact commander," says Protector in a mechanical voice. Epsilon gave one curt nod of approval. His batteries were a newer model, and able to hold much higher power units.

The girls were all sitting with their backs in a row and aliens were now all seated waiting for their attempt at choosing their bride. Epsilon was not interested in the human species if it were not for the prophecy. He wanted to give a child from out of his blood. Epsilon sat down weighing his heavy body on a wooden chair and waiting for the proceeding to start. He could see anxiety clouding the faces of many aliens and their horns looking brittle and droopy with rings visible around them.

"We are here to start the auction on the young fertile girls. Whoever bids the highest becomes the owner of the girl and, she, his rightful bride to be taken to the land of Drexicons," says the host, talking through a large cone-shaped speaker and every hair on Epsilon's body raised to attention.

"And what about the scar mark in the inner thigh," asks an alien impatiently from among the audience. For a human female must have a scar, to have the magic child. Scar or not, Epsilon wanted a bride.

"We cannot show the scar and it is up to your fortune," says the announcer in a growling voice.

The tension rises in the room and everyone becomes alert. It was a high bet to find a suitable mate and pay a high price. But what if she doesn't have a scar? The questions were many in the minds of aliens. The auction attendees were handpicked chiefs of Drexicon with enough power and strength to afford to buy a human bride.

The lights go out and the room gets dark when the first girl is presented. All gazes were fixed on her and she stood timidly in the center of the wooden stage. It was made from thin wood planks. It was not a glorious stage, but served it's purpose to give the Drexicons a view of their purchase.

No one in the room could see her legs shaking and her lips trembling despite the temperature being so hot. The magenta dress clung tightly to her thin frame and her hair was tightly tied in a top bun. She turns around to show her assets and move in a circle like an animal in the circus.

No sound kills the silence in the room and she keeps standing there like a statue waiting for someone to make an offer on her.

Silence.

Silence prevails and the girl keeps standing unwanted and undesired by the Drexicon males, who didn't even flinch or make a move. After a long pause of what seems like a million seconds, the host asks the girl to exit the stage. She will never be able to enter the auction again and her fate of becoming a chief's bride is ever laid to rest with continuous juggles of hunger and dreadfulness in the human camp. Tears roll down her cheeks and if she finds herself super unwanted and utterly useless in the room.

Five girls were left and now the anticipation in the room grew further.

"Will I even get a bride today?" Epsilon questions himself while looking at the ground. This was a place beyond his life experiences when he was so busy with his voyages and defeating humans, one after another, on their soil that he never slightly thought about marriage. And here he was with all his precious belongings to pay for a woman, just a woman.

Epsilon was so busy in his introspection that he didn't realize that the next girl was standing on the stage and he could hear men raising their voices and quoting money for her. Their bids rose higher and higher. The room was loud with shouting.

Epsilon casually looked at the stage and his heart skipped a beat and he suddenly stood up from his chair. His eyes locked on hers.

Clad in red and looking at the audience with her big kohled eyes she looked like a fairy from paradise. She was the female he saw a million times in his dreams. And she left him so many times in his nightmares. The same person in flesh and bone. Strangely standing in the middle of the show.

"Moon," says Epsilon while not blinking his eyes at all. He heard her name in his dreams and called her too. She never listened to him like a deaf princess on her strange voyage.

"One million battery units," Epsilon shouts, in a hurry when all gazes look at him in awe and surprise.

"One million for just a woman?" Asks another chief trying to put some mind in his brain.

"Yes," says Epsilon with a tone so firm that all the chiefs resign their cards in their laps.

Other Drexicons thought it was super insane and stupid to bet like that. Epsilon could be crazy. But he didn't think he lost his mind to bet so high at the auction table. There could be an equal possibility of the female being barren or scarless as well.

It was a gamble Epsilon was willing to take.

Moon looks at Epsilon in disbelief and then starts walking slowly from her point fixated under her feet. The host took Moon by hand and brought her to Epsilon with a large grin plastered all across his face. If all their women could be sold at this price, then they could easily defeat these gruesome and cruel Drexicon aliens. It was the perfect plan.

Aunt Lexicon received applause for grooming Moon so well. But she knew that Moon needed nothing of her expertise. She had taught her different moves, positions, and acts of lovemaking. And Lexicon believed truly that Moon will prove to be a dangerous submissive wife in bed.

The Protector produced the batteries from out the large bag and handed it over to the announcer. The announcer scanned them, to verify that they were charged.

Epsilon was so busy looking at his bride. And now he wanted to see her from up close and his heart skipped a beat again and all the blood started running down to his groin. He felt he would come right there, looking at the woman of his dreams. She was beautiful, soft and timid. Moon was full of curves and Epsilon couldn't wait to see his purchase in the flesh.

Moon didn't look up at Epsilon, and kept looking at the ground seemingly confused and utterly nervous. Epsilon wanted to rip off her clothes and make animalistic love to her right there and then in the middle of the room like a hungry beast. She left him so wanting in his dreams that now he felt no control over his emotions.

"Let's go," he says gruffly, in a hurry while holding Moon's hand

and quickly dragging her out of the beacon.

Epsilon wanted to reach his city soon and hug his mate for hours. His body was hungry for her for years and now he realized his yearning which he never felt before. He forgot all about the want of a child and all he could think of was this female with him.

Moon was following Epsilon looking at his dark eyes and large body and she felt so small, weak, and helpless in front of him. Even her hands just got lost in his big giant palm and she kept clutching to his hand like a small child.

The whole journey swiftly passed in silence sitting on the back of the horse with the warrior and Moon was not sure what the future held for her but she felt calm and protected. Holding on to the back of her alien, his presence gave her confidence and it felt good.

He was the most good-looking man she ever saw in her life and even catching a little glimpse of him from under her fluttering eyelashes made her immensely shy. All Lady Lexicon's lessons started evaporating out of her brain and she felt stupid and unsure at the same time. The horse was galloping at high speed and her big boobs bounced and rubbed against Epsilon's back. Moon felt horny and desire rushed through her body like a bolt of light. She never touched a man let alone sit with him with her boobs and sex rubbing on his back.

The hormones of euphoria, need and rush spiraling through her body making her ache in between her legs. She lightly touched her finger in the center of her legs. And felt so wet that for a moment she thought that she had accidentally peed. It was not pee but her body reacting to the hot man riding the horse like a cheetah.

He was hers now—forever, Moon thought with a little smile dancing on her lips and holding the grip tight on her enormous alien. She let her fingers gingerly explore his body. His stature was large and muscular, unlike anything Moon had ever experienced.

Moon didn't realize that Epsilon was outrageously crazy hard for her, as she accidently grazed his tented cock.

"Watch your hands little female, before I fuck you in the grass."

Epsilon was on the verge of taking her down from the horse and fucking her hard on the soft soil. But it took him a lot of restraint to control himself.

They reached their cozy tent in the middle of the large army base camp and Epsilon almost dragged Moon inside the camp.

"Wait, slow down," Moon whimpered as Epsilon dragged her in the tent.

His emotions were running high like he was drunk and intoxicated by the beauty of that voluptuous human female.

"Stand here still," says Epsilon looking down at her. She looked apprehensive in front of him yet so powerful with her dark sexy gaze and long black hair. Similar to an enchantress from a distant world.

At that moment Epsilon Kristos wanted to rub his dick on her lips, which were so full. He could ejaculate for hours on her pretty face. This female made him want to do crazy things he never even thought of doing ever.

Epsilon lights some fire from his magic stick and lights the candle. The soft warm glow of the candle vividly lightens the atmosphere in the tent and the heavy thick air of desire lingers between the alien-man and his seductive human female.

Moon stood still like a statue completely intimidated by her man and feeling so weak in her legs. His hot gaze made her feel shy as no man ever touched her or came close to her.

Epsilon was now standing in front of her, sinking in her long red dress.

"Take off your clothes," says Epsilon with a command in his tone.

Moon looked at him stunned, as she only uttered a few words till now. And now she expected to be friends with him first and then enter into a more intimate relationship. But she knew the drill Aunt Lexicon taught her so well. Moon knew the effect men had after looking at her. So she was confident in making him hers forever.

Moon quickly took off her shirt exposing her red bra and matching net panties. As she moves down the white swelling sides of her boobs start to show off from out her bra. The thin see-through net was unable to cover her full boobs and the sweet soft flesh made its way out from the edges.

Epsilon couldn't help a constant need to rip her lingerie and thrash her body down and suck all the milk out of her large boobs, if it was there. He was so hungry for her. And she didn't even know how sensationally sexy she was. Though he held his breath patiently and kept ogling at her.

Epsilon closed his eyes for a moment and opened them again to look at her with a clouded gaze.

She was standing naked in front of him now in her lacy red bra which was so thin that he could see her nipples pushing out and erect just like his own hard cock. Her panties looked a little wet and Epsolin moved forward and slipped his finger in her soft wet pussy through the side of her panties not taking them off. The act ran sensations through his body and he closed his eyes for an instant to revel at the moment.

"Ahhhhh," escapes a sensuous sound from out of Moon's lips and that was the first sound he heard from out her mouth and it was the most beautiful in the world, full of a lot of carnal promises and pleasure.

Epsilon kept moving his finger in and out while seeing her moaning and standing at his mercy. She was so tight. And so wet. And a virgin. With her hymen coming in the way of his finger.

"I'm going to push into you now," Epsilon said, "it will hurt, only for a moment."

"Please," Moon said in a pleading tone. "I'm a virgin." She sucked in a deep breath. Little drops of blood made his finger red as he broke her hymen and could see a shadow of pain crossing her lovely face and she winced for a moment. Epsilon felt a pinch in his heart like her pain. It pained him too, but he could never confess it to her.

"Breathe in through your nose," he instructed, "deeply." Moon closed her eyes in pain. If these were only his fingers... He thought human females were more elastic, to accommodate large Drexicon cocks.

"Ok," Moon sighed.

"In time, you will learn to enjoy this."

Epsilon was an alien — a fierce Drexicon. And he had to act like a warrior in front of this female who took his breath away in millions of ways. Long before he even knew she existed and long after he knew that he loved her without ever seeing her.

Epsilon wanted to fuck her hard but also understood that she needed time to adjust to his very large cock, similar to the size of a hard iron fist, and it was better to loosen her hole with his skilled fingers first. Epsilon had tried fucking some Drexicon females before and he knew the anatomy of making their holes larger. But they were all so rigid and manly, like abnormal males, and they could not come closer to the plump soft pussy of Moon, her long silky hair, her soft pink lips, and her round perfect ass.

Though his cock could never enter the rigid holes of Drexicon females and he was technically a virgin too; never having a fuck-time with anything alive and breathing. And this female unmanned him and made him so fragile in his body that he fears losing himself in front of her.

He gained control over his emotions again. A woman so seductively enchanting could only be found in Epsilon's dreams and he wanted to fuck her a million times each day till eternity. Ahhh. He wished.

Again, looking at her and sinking in her beauty in while feeling the large lump of emotions in his throat Epsilon kept maneuvering her hole. This female was completely deluding his thoughts, but he had to remember his goal of making a 'magic (love) child,' to fulfill his needs of roaring through all the upcoming battles and tightly and firmly plant the flag of Drexicons on the human soil.

"Let me look at you." The next moment Epsilon ripped off her panties and bras in one swift motion and her big breasts fell open and bounced in front of him ready to please his hungry mouth.

Moon felt so shy but she didn't dare cover herself because she didn't want to upset her mate.

He let out a sultry chuckle.

"You don't have be scared little human, I will keep my dick in your pussy and scar you so you don't feel much pain," says Epsilon, and Moon groans again feeling an aching need in her wet pussy to feel him, his skin and his dick making her feel full.

Epsilon orders her to lie down on the floor and brings the candle, he just lit a few moments back, alongside him while sitting down. Epsilon took off his clothes and wore a loose cloth around his cock as it was impossible to contain his cock in any pants at that time. His erection was distracting him and his mind was completely numbed.

"Open your legs wide and I will tie your hands to the back of the bamboo pole," says Epsilon.

Moon felt scared and she didn't know what was about to happen to her. But she trusted this man. This alien. Her new forever mate. And something in his tone of his voice made her feel that he madly loved her. Though she was not sure.

Epsilon ties her hands tightly to the pole and stretched her legs towards him facing, her pussy in front of him just a few inches away from his mouth and he could just stretch his neck and easily lick her pink flesh, so he rubs her clitoris gently with his thumb while flickering his tongue on her wet sex, listening to the sweet hums of her moans. He could see that she was ready and horny and he kept fucking her with three fingers now to make room for his dick while gently squeezing her clitoris.

"Are you ready mate? It will pain a little," he asks while wanting to pain her, and hear her screams loud and clear. Something about her screams made him feel so powerful and aroused. And it will be an announcement for the whole Drexicon society that she belonged to him and him alone.

"Yes," says Moon not knowing what else to say.

A tradition Drexicons so staunchly followed, in which the screams meant a true belonging of the female to her partner on the wedding night and no other Drexicon male could dare to look at her. Gazing at the female with lustful eyes could result in his death. Epsilon wanted her screams to gash through the roofs up till the skies and every single element on earth knows that she belongs to him.

Epsilon grabs his cock from under his pants and rubs the tip on her wet pussy, and before she even realizes he enters inside her fully not being able to wait any further.

"Arghhhh..."

It was painful for Moon. She was wet, she wanted it, although she knew it would hurt her.

"Arch your back and keep your butt in the air," he gruffly says while grunting and pushing his dick deep inside her. The depths he could reach, vanishing in the dark abyss of her mystic world.

With each thrust, he was exploring her, her senses, and the subjective parts of her existence she didn't know existed. She becomes an embodiment of sensations, a toy in his hands, and his one move made her scream louder with extreme exotic pleasure. For Moon, it was the perfect cocktail of painful pleasure ripping through her body and entering through her soul reaching the heights of pleasures unimaginable.

Epsilon was rubbing all her moist spots inside her body and she was writhing beneath him, unable to move or flex her hips.

Epsilon was looking at her every move, each minuscule sound leaving her pink lips and the rise and fall in her well-measured breasts. He grabbed her nipple with one hand while continuing to fuck her hard.

"Ahhh," she moans heavily. A loud shriek leaves Moon's lips and Epsilon puts his large hand on her mouth and keeps moving inside her at a good pace.

He closes his eyes for a moment to savor what he was

experiencing. It was heaven inside her. Tight heaven and the pleasure he felt in his body were unexplainable while he kept rubbing her clitoris. Moon was so full and she didn't know how empty she was before. And her body was quivering with pleasure when she felt a hot sensation on her inner thigh.

Epsilon was fucking her pushing his dick further inside her and also scaring her with hot candle liquid. She did not have a scar on her inner thigh, so Epsilon was giving one to her. It was a part of the tradition.

It was a heady mix of pain and pleasure and she couldn't even move. She had to absorb all the sensations all at once.

Epsilon fucked her so hard, he drove Moon into the ground. His cock was thicker than her wrist and she felt like her whole body belonged to this handsome man now who was rocking her hard and so ravenous for her.

The hot liquid, the burn sensation and her large orgasm all exploded at once and for a moment. Everything went blank in front of Moon's eyes and she felt like she was flying up into the heavens.

They both orgasmed together with their animalistic shrieks in the night, alarming the horses outside of the tent, because of their rough lovemaking. They didn't make their magic child and were short on time. Per the prophecy, they only had 600 seconds to orgasm simultaneously.

But it was just the beginning. And Epsilon's Moon was successfully scarred.....

CHAPTER 3

"YOUR PAIN WRENCHES MY HEART BUT FEEDS MY SOUL WITH CARNAL PLEASURE"

"I love your butt all red and hanging in the air waiting for my next spank"

Epsilon Kristos was tired looking strangely at the black clouds moving towards him, his fists clenched and his heart beating fast. He needed a release of energy and he could feel tiny beads of sweat sliding tenderly at the back of his shoulders and reaching down in his pants.

"I need her," growled Epsilon with fists tightly shut.

He turned around and took swift long strides to reach Moon, his little human. Her soft rhythmic snores dwelling in his ears and him thinking about her sound asleep last night. And he looked at her the whole night not being able to sleep at all. Other days he would sleep all tangled with her body. He felt more motivated to work and his dreams about a future Drexicon's empire more strong and more vivid than ever. Epsilon daydreamed about her all day and at night he would sleep soundly in her arms or look at her beautiful face for endless hours.

His body was on fire with desire seeping in every vein of his body and his full lips widened in awe and passion showing a glimpse of his white even teeth. He didn't remember the life when Moon wasn't here and his auction bride had no existence. And a chilling thought of his nightmares shuddered him.

"Mate, where are you?" He shouts from afar while playing with the edge of his weapon. He anticipated her with wide legs open, waiting and waiting for him. But he knew that she couldn't hear him from afar and he didn't want her to be seen by Drexicon males before she fall fully pregnant with their child.

He told her this much that whenever he is out on a voyage for long, she should know that he must be hungry to enter inside her and she should wear her thin filmy satin silk dress only which makes her nipples protruding and visible pushing against her dress and she should be lying with her legs wide and open for him to enter inside her fast. And her misconduct could lead to serious repercussions and punishments.

"When the sun sets, your place should be in bed with her hands resting on your breasts," says Epsilon. He made the matters of mating sound professional to her like a task or a job they needed to do to make children and the only reason for which he bought her.

But he knew deep within the dark folds of his heart that he needed her not for the sake of heavy fuck. His heart burned and desired for her and there was something always smoldering within him which made him reclaim and possess her and every single cell of her body and to go on distance traveling within her body. She was his.

Ahh, what sweet thoughtful escapades in his brain and all the sensitive points in his body come alive, alert, and to attend to his wayward thoughts and he keeps walking in the jungle and the camps with a heavy visible bulge in his pants. There was no cooling off and he couldn't hide it as well.

Epsilon's thoughts took him to remember Moon's auburn eyes widening with shock at his instructions to lay waiting in bed and his heart melted like soft mushy butter while looking at her. He didn't know if he loved her. Or if looking at her made his heart swell. But no one ever discussed Love in the alien world. The alien concept of emotions never fully struck him. All he knew was war, weapons, ritualistic mating and being in more numbers than humans.

Epsilon wanted a better world. And all could come true if the magic human was born, and born fast otherwise Drexicons could reach extinction like dinosaurs.

Epsilon's speed grew in momentum and he wanted to reach Moon. His want for her was evident from the large bulge in his pants and he needed the fog to shed to focus on his hunting mission with Aeryn. The hunting was important as the clouds signaled rain and they calculated on their beeping machine about the upcoming rain spell.

Large heaps of beef and canned tomatoes had to be prepared and stored nicely to keep the Drexicons in good muscular strength.

"Why are you in a hurry Epsilon? The things for the voyage are ready," asks Aeryn from afar, trying to catch his attention while holding a basket full of things, while fingering a hunting gun neatly wrapped around his big torso.

"I will tell you later," Epsilon growls, not in a mood to discuss further and thanking in heart to see his tent in sight. The idea of Moon with legs open on their bed, all wet in her pussy and moaning with carnal pleasure makes Epsilon super horny and his big knob feels trapped inside his pants ready to be fully out and deep inside Moon's wet heaven.

"Ahhhh," he grunts at the delight and pressure in his pants and reaches the door slamming it open.

He could see his beloved nowhere which added a fury of disappointment and Epsilon felt a lump in his throat. He expected his little human to obey him and have the stamina to feel his rock-hard cock inside her for hours.

How would she be able to grant him the magic child otherwise?

"Moon," says Epsilon, while taking off his shirt.

His physique was so tall and beautiful that he could easily win the utterly 'most desirable man on the lands of planets,' contest without anyone falling near his charm. He was muscular, large and chiseled with handsome features.

He waited for two seconds and before he could take a step to find her, he saw her coming out with her long curly hair falling loose on her back and she was wearing a net shirt with everything visible underneath.

Her long legs, flawless and white, and her black panties fit nicely on them.

Epsilon moved forward and grabbed her nipple in his thumb and squeezed it hard which made Moon mewl under his touch. The brown nipples were visible from under her red attire and he could easily grab them and rub them hard making her wet in her panties.

"I told you to wait for me with open legs, didn't I?" he asks with fury ringing in his voice.

"I am sorry commander, I went to use the bathroom," says Moon in a meak voice looking straight in his dark eyes.

She was stunning with long lashes and auburn eyes and her curves voluptuous nicely fitting in Epsilon's big hands. He could easily knead and squeeze her breasts for hours and milk them to quench his inner animalistic thirst.

"I will have to spank you for your misconduct," he growls, with a command in his voice.

Epsilon loved spanking her and hearing her screams fed his inner wilderness. His inner and deepest carnal desires. Her reactions fed his primal urge to dominate her. He needed to dominate every ounce of her being. Her mind, body and soul.

Her screams and moans kept following him during the days at work when he would be surrounded by his commandos. He missed her in every moment of his day and wished to carry her everywhere he would go.

"Undress first," Epsilon gruffly commands, while ripping-off her flimsy lingerie. With his one swift movement, the dress and the panties fall apart and Moon stands naked and wet in front of him. She didn't dare cover her shame with her hands because she knew that it would add to his fury.

Her dark black hair fell to the front giving her a seductive and ethereal look.

Epsilon wanted to take her there and then and release the fog from his brain but he needed to punish her so she always understands the importance of his orders.

"Turn around and lean on the table," Epsilon commanded in a hoarse voice, sinking his fingers in her raw beauty.

"I never saw a female so beautiful and sexy at the same time," thinks Epsilon, while parting her legs with his strong hands.

Her behind was so beautiful and soft like bundles of cashmere cotton where he could bury his face and lick her moist liquids leaking out of her soft hole.

He rubs her back gently and opens her legs further, while standing in between her legs.

"I will spank you ten times, count with me," Epsilon says, in an alarming tone to make her anticipate his blows.

"One," he says while hardly blowing his hand on her rear and consciously smacking her pussy from behind to tease her clitoris. She was completely naked and exposed leaning on the table helplessly in front of him. And he felt like the most powerful man in the world in possession of this angelic beauty.

"Ahhhh," a large scream of pain and pleasure exits Moon's lips and, she writhes beneath the hot contact of his hand and her hips.

She didn't dare ask him to fill her with his rock hard cock inside her. As she badly wanted to feel full with his big thick cock.

"Two," another smack touches the cheek of her hips and she feels a build-up inside her. Moon was so horny that she was scared to come the next time he spanked her hard.

"Why does this punishment make me so full of painful pleasure?" Moon asks, while holding the edges of the table tightly in her grip.

He let out a sultry chuckle. "Because you're a good girl."

Epsilon couldn't hold his desires any longer. He slowly pulled down the zipper of his pants to free his cock and rub it on the wet pussy of his mate. He wanted to slam it hard inside her, but he needed to finish her punishment.

"Ten," he counts, with the smack of his palm, while quickly entering inside her in full force rubbing the inside of her sweet spot.

"Arghhh," screams Moon and his screams so loud that the whole camp must have heard her.

"You need to come in ten minutes, Moon," says Epsilon while rocking her slowly now holding on tight to her small waist.

He wanted to change his position as she was so hot from this angle and Moon couldn't resist coming in less than a minute. He quickly retreated his cock leaving her all empty and unfulfilled while gently rubbing her ass as well to soothe his heavy blows. He kept rubbing her rear for some time while cooling off his cock, but there was no cooling off while looking at the woman of his dreams. But he never told her this much.

"Turn around," Epsilon orders, and Moon suddenly turns around while facing him now. Her eyes meet his and he feels a tug on his heart.

"You remember that we need to prolong it," Epsilon says while needing an answer from her.

"I hope you remember your punishment and will never disobey me again," he says while quickly adding the phrase to his previous sentence.

"Yes Commander," Moon says, while feeling a little nervous in her heart.

She didn't tell him that she won't be able to hold out for long as she felt so horny, looking at her big muscular man with well-cut biceps and lean stomach. The sight of his long thick cock was enough to make her come in her dreams. She wanted to touch him there and take him in his mouth sucking on him for hours. But she didn't dare say anything.

She felt so shy and a little scared of him too. Though she loved his smell. And loved when he wrapped his arms around her body at night. And she loved when he rested his head on her breasts early in the mornings. She loved everything about her alien.

Epsilon grabbed Moon from behind, lifting her legs in the air while widening his tight lips and rubbing the tip of his cock on her wet flesh.

He slowly enters inside her and feels blood rushing from his brain, to his cock.

This was a pleasure he never experienced before. Pure bliss...

"Your pussy is so wet and tight," Epsilon rasps, while adjusting his big cock in her tight hole and pushing it hard until it's fully inside her. He rocks it hardly now grabbing the ankle of her legs firmly and fucking her for what seemed like hours.

They both screamed with the painful pleasure of their orgasm and Epsilon pulled his cock out, wanting to ejaculate some of his semen on her breasts.

It was a pleasurable attempt but not one where they could make their magic baby.

"Only pure bliss," thinks Epsilon, while licking his semen on her big juicy nipples and sucking them hard.

He could fuck her all night.

"I never seem to get enough of you," Epsilon says, while kissing her on the lips, one last time before leaving for his voyage.

"I will be back soon," he says while sucking her lips.

He was still inside her and Moon couldn't tell him that she would miss him, and she felt empty without him, in her body and this tent.

She would miss his smell and everything about him. She didn't dare say. And she thought that she would come again while he was sucking her lips with full throttle. She flexes her hips and Epsilon couldn't resist to fuck her again.

Though he needed to fuck her underwater next time to prolong her orgasm.

"I need the baby fast to secure my throne," thinks Epsilon before his second orgasm and sprawling and covering the small body of his most beautiful treasure.

CHAPTER 4

I AM A TERRITORIAL ALIEN MAN WHO ASSERTS HIS CLAIM FROM YOUR INLETS

"My heart bled when I saw you bleeding"

Y ou are our soldiers and we will wait for the signals," the memory of Aunt Lexicon's voice rang in Moon's ears and she didn't know what was expected of her to do.

Since Moon came into the camp, she saw not a single alien coming near her and all she saw was Epsilon Kristos, her quenchless handsome alien mate.

Moon had to prepare the meat for supper. Then get ready to wait in bed before her alien arrived. But pain was growing in her back and she couldn't drag herself out of bed. She couldn't bring Epsilon's wrath on herself who clearly demanded her to be fuck-ready with a piping hot meal served on the table before sunset.

He craved her and then food after a long tiring day in the jungles and war fields, hunting, with his commandos. His appetite always called to make love to her first and then eat the food from her hands. He loved enslaving her, making her sit in a relaxed pose and finger her from the back or bring a shimmering stick to slap her on her butt.

He demanded all the kinky joys to feed his barren soul and expected her to submit to his desires, which Moon happily did because whatever he did to her body just stretched her horizon to experience more hunger-filled love.

He loved her and that was so visible from the way he looked in her eyes, from the way he kissed her tasting her tongue, and from the way a painful expression crossed his face clouding his expression when she felt pain but he never confessed his love rather always hid it behind his staunch demeanor.

Moon felt wet thinking about all the sweet memories with her alien while putting some meat in the sauteed onions. She felt wetter than usual and got up from the tiny wooden stool after putting the meat on the stove and noticed tiny drops of blood on the floor.

"Ohhh!" She gasps out of sheer terror.

Moon started bleeding. She was on her period which meant that she didn't become pregnant. And she couldn't give sex to Epsilon. Which he demanded each day and his becoming furious ran a shiver down Moon's spine. Her heart sank to the daunting idea and she clutched her clothes out of sheer fear. Her heart thumped in her chest and she didn't know what to do.

"Let me wear my panties first," Moon says, turning all white with terror in her heart.

Moon sat in the bathroom for longer than usual, putting a tampon deep inside her vagina and thinking of what to say to Epsilon. She picked a lilac loose dress to wear which covered her whole body.

She laid down in the bed after putting her hair in a tight bun. Moon scrunches her eyes and wanted to bury herself deep in the blanket.

"Will I be able to carry his child?" She asks, and remembers Aunt Lexicon telling her to fall pregnant the first month. Her education couldn't make her get pregnant though she followed all her instructions religiously. But she and Epsilon couldn't time their orgasm or follow the six hundred rule well.

Moon was thinking when she heard the familiar bang on the door and the in next moment, she saw Epsilon hovering over her. His handsome face looked closely at Moon. She was cowering under his large stature. His eyes bore deep in her soul.

"How are you?" Epsilon asks, in a low voice.

It was unlike him to ask her but somehow, he sensed something different or pale about her.

"I'm okay," she manages to say, while not feeling anywhere near okay.

"Stand up," he orders.

Moon stands up while trying to not fall off her feet. Her pain was less but she felt weak due to the stress.

"What should I do?" The same question again rumbles through her brain.

"Take off your shirt," he says while looking squarely at her.

Epsilon looked every inch a handsome commander in his khaki attire, with a square-shaped machine hanging on the side of his pocket. It always hung there and Moon didn't know the function of it.

Moon took off the single shirt she wore, and she anticipated the dreadful moment to inch closer.

She wore a pale blue cotton net bra and panties. Epsilon approved front-open bras to quickly unhook them and stick his mouth on her nipples. He felt that she looked a little distressed and reluctant though he kept staring at her.

Moon stood straight with her bra and panties and a bun of her hair on top of her crown while trying not to look at him. But to look somewhere in a distant point.

Epsilon came closer and elevated her face to look at her and kiss her lightly on her forehead. He doesn't ask her to remove her panties or bra and keeps standing in close proximity to her.

"Sit down," he says in her ear like a tiny, firm whisper.

Moon quickly sits down thanking her guardian angels that he didn't ask her to strip.

"Pull my pants down and take me in your mouth," he says while intently looking at her.

He always startled her and made her pulse throb hard, with his different commands. This time was no different and she felt all the blood rush to the apex juncture of her legs, wanting to hold him and suck him forever. She wanted to touch him there and touch all his body. But could never muster enough courage or gather more strength to ask. All their lovemaking happened with her hands tied or restrained away from her. She never got a full glimpse of his heavy cock and now he wants her to hold it and take it in her mouth.

Ahhh, it felt so hot and so freaking powerful at the same time holding her alien in her hands and her sweet wet mouth slurping on his hard meat and drinking his yummy fluids tripping out of his slit, while looking up at him to see his intoxicating reactions.

Moon sat down with bent knees and unzipped his pants and pull out his colossal and hard cock (ever-so-ready-for-her) and looked up at him with a nervous glance. Epsilon was keenly looking down at her wanting her to quickly put her tongue on his flesh but he waited to see her move. She holds his cock in her full fist from the base and starts sucking his balls.

"Ahhhhh, oh my...." exclaims Epsilon while closing his eyes. He didn't expect the sudden uproar of nerves impacting up to his brain like some drug fusing his mind and he pushes his hips forward wanting her to take him all in her mouth.

She doesn't disappoint and starts licking the tip of his cock running her tongue down and slowly blowing on his dick with her mouth. It was a proper hot puff of air releasing her mouth mixed with sticky saliva liberally poured, and he felt multiple sensations blowing the nerves around his shaft and all the veins becoming ever so prominent on his cock.

The veins running full of blood and nerves exploded his body like a road map of sensations and he felt goosebumps on his body and tingling pricks at the base of his nape. This was beyond real and not even dreamy but a freaking bizarre mind-blowing reality.

Epsilon closed his eyes to relish the moment and then slowly peek at her while she was hardly and religiously sucking on his cock...

Epsilon couldn't decide at that moment what was more pleasurable? Having getting sucked by her mouth or fucking her hard...But he wanted the moment to never end and stay in her mouth endlessly. Unceasingly.

His brain was in no state to ponder over serious questions and he basked again in the glory of the most pleasurable moment of his life.

Epsilon gently rubbed his horns to feel double the euphoria and felt like the most powerful man while seeing his cock in the mouth of his human. He quickly grabbed her hair with one hand to see her evil charm while she worked her tongue and mouth on his cock, and peeked up at him.

Epsilon wanted to freeze and garnish that moment forever in his brain of her sitting on the floor in a powder blue bra and panties excessively showing her cleavage and waves of cascades of hair falling down her neck, keeping her lips round and tight on his big fat cock.

Epsilon saw her sucking his cock as she worshiped him. And she was holding and carefully sucking a hard-earned possession. He was her possession and her obsession which she adored but was too afraid to tell. He was floating and drowning in the irony of that climax and he forcefully came in her mouth not trying to hold a single drop of his semen back.

"Taste me, Moon," Epsilon says, while slowly pulling out his cock and squirting ropes of his semen all across her face and on her cleavage. It was a powerful orgasm, but his business with Moon wasn't over. He didn't just finish on her face.

Epsilon's cock hardened again. He wanted to fuck Moon in her deep dark cavity. His place of heaven and desire. His obsession and his place of sanctuary from everything worldly known to him.

"Take off your panties and bra," Epsilon commands. Moon had to face this dreadful moment now.

"Iiii, umm, actuallyyy," Moon stammers and looks at him helplessly with tears rolling down her cheeks and the semen still wet on her face.

Epsilon feels anger pumping in his body at her delay. He makes her stand up and rips off her bra and panties in seconds making her all naked. He sees a cloth pad full of blood falling to the ground but doesn't say anything.

"Open your legs," he commands with rage and his eyes turning red.

"I ammm bleedingggg," says Moon out of sheer protest.

Epsilon doesn't say anything. He picked up her bra and tied it tightly on her mouth, so she couldn't speak anymore.

"You have talked enough," he says, and goes away to get something.

After a couple of minutes, Epsilon comes back with a small bottle in his hand, and uses it to force open Moon's legs.

He leisurely drops something slimy and oily on Moon's weeping asshole and rubs it with his fingers, massaging her there for some time. And then pushes his finger in her ass. She writhes under this new territorial invasion but cannot protest anything because she already made him angry enough.

"I will take you from the back," announces Epsilon, while positioning his cock's head on her ever-so-tight asshole, and slowly starts to pump inside. The lube helps him find his way while he plunges one of his fingers into her bleeding pussy.

He was fucking her in two holes and Moon felt so full. In her stomach like all her hunger being driven away once for all and her empty holes finally meeting their missing part.

Epsilon picks up some pace with lots of lube making it easy to go deep in her and quickly shifts her around and makes her sit backward in his lap.

He holds Moon's weight on his hands and directs her ass to rock on his cock. Her ass goes deep on his cock in the sitting position.

They find momentum and Moon finds it so intimate while sitting and riding his cock, in her ass and rubbing her pussy from the front. Her plump breasts were jumping up and down, while her mouth was still tight with her bra, absorbing all her moans.

"Now turn around and place your feet on my thighs," Epsilon commands, while taking out his cock from her ass.

Moon does as commanded and places both of her feet on his

thighs, while he slips his cock in her asshole. Moon starts to fall, so Epsilon firmly holds her in place, grasping her hips. Her pussy and ass were fully exposed and now he had a front view of her body. It was a beautiful sight.

Moon slowly went up and down, feeling the big entry in her back hole, while her front hole was fully stretched out with his fingers. Epsilon saw a drop of warm fluid rolling out of her vagina. Moon held his legs and now started riding him, while Epsilon fingered her with one hand and caressed her nipples with the other.

It was long unexpected lovemaking for them in the harshest ways. And Moon wanted to come a million times, while her back hole stretched open for her handsome alien.

Epsilon was close and he saw Moon's eyes closing so he grabbed both breasts and squeezed her tits, which undid her and she could not hold back her orgasm any longer.

"Ahh," she shrieked under the soft cotton bra, and came, and came with her sweet spots trembling with pleasure. Moon collapsed on Epsilon's Chest. He came in her ass and what a mighty act that was. She was completely filled.

They both felt fully satisfied and fell into a deep slumber resting naked. Epsilon's cock was still inside her. The magic child wasn't made, but Epsilon conquered another territory of hers and she was all his. All her holes belonged to him and him alone. They were his last thoughts before slipping into a deep sleep.

But Moon was on a mission that she didn't remember. And

Epsilon was on a mission which he didn't remember. They both needed to remember or they could lose each other to the dark cruel world. Somewhere far away, the human soldiers were tracking them and Moon didn't know that her life could be in danger if she didn't help them with their advances.

She slept so peacefully in her alien's arms and the danger was clouding their peace from outside, keeping a stronghold and checking on them........which they were oblivious to at the moment cocooning in their bubble of passion.

CHAPTER 5

KEEP LOOKING IN MY EYES AND FEEL MY BURNING DESIRE TO RULE OVER EVERY IMPACT ON YOUR SOUL

"The moment of an enchanted miracle is hatched"

It had been two months since the auction and there was complete silence in the Drexicon camp during the ceasefire and temporary stop on wars with the humans. It seemed like the war had started from within and every chief was silently working hard to make the magic child. Twenty women were auctioned in the event and Epsilon didn't miss a chance to fuck his bride ever since. But they couldn't fulfill all the conditions and the rumors were clear that no chief or Drexicon warrior achieved near to the proposed conditions in the camp. Carefully made timers of 600 seconds were placed in each camp and the race was on to conceive the child as the prophecy could be fulfilled for only one child. Epsilon wasn't clear on how the men scarred their females, but his Moon was nicely scarred in between her vagina and ass while his cock rested inside her making her forget about the hot candle liquid scarring her skin. His cock rose to full attention, again at the slightest thought of Moon and he vowed in his heart to make her pregnant today to find a better future and more power for themselves.

The door fell open and there she was lying on her back. Fully naked. Epsilon approved the bold move and slowly reached to her while kissing the back of her neck. He moved her to get on her front and rubbed his index finger on her lips making them all white under his hard friction.

"Be ready to hold onto your orgasm for 600 seconds Moon," he says alarmingly while placing his mouth on her two wet lips, and sitting in between her legs making room for himself with his legs.

He Kissed her fervently on the lips, parting them with his tongue and sliding his tongue in her sweet mouth. With all the hunger and power and shoving his tongue in her mouth and tasting her all, sucking the energy out of her mouth. Sucking on her juices like a hungry wild zombie ready to drink in all her blood, while rocking his cock inside her. He had carefully wrapped all her hair around his fist, and wrapped her waist in his other arm.

"Look at me. I'm going to taste your pussy," he says while kissing her, stunning Moon with his phrase. He was a lion awakened out of his den hungry for her juices and all her wet liquids pouring from every inch of her body. Epsilon wanted to get fully drenched in her fluids.

"Do humans also crave to lick a cunt?" thinks Moon, while trying to match his dance of the tongue he played so passionately in between her wet folds. This man fucked her every day or sometimes twice a day like she is the only female in the world. He dazzled her each time with his immense energy and his appetite for her.

He took Moon's all conscious sensibilities away and it was the first time that he kissed her on her wet lips, long after making frantic

60

love to her and she felt strangely loved and hungry at the same time, tugging her fingers in his hair pinning his head in place and wanting this kiss, this union and his feel inside her to linger on forever.

"Don't move," commands Epsilon while turning his attention to suck her clit. He felt some juices filling his mouth. He lapped at her cunt, licking all the slick away.

Epsilon felt like a wild beast with an animal instinct to fuck his mate and being inside her makes him forget everything and anything and he would belong at the moment forever. The moments kept piling and freezing in his mind ready to haunt him all through the day. He couldn't confess it in front of his alien warriors that Moon dominated his thoughts, her sweet little moans turning into large cries, and her soft tender breasts made him rock hard through the day and he would wish to have wings to fly and make love to her as many times as infinity. Once she screamed his name, he mounted her once more.

This female kept increasing his desire for her, never quite putting an end to it. Each time he saw her, he saw an added passion simmering in his heart. He didn't even know what to do with all those passions for his little human. He had strong feelings for his female.

The only way he knew to release all his energy was to ejaculate long and hard inside her soft wet pussy. Ahhh...He came back to the moment fucking her harder and moving inside her as a heavy meaty boner fully fixed and belonging inside a hole, a hole that fitted him so perfectly and tight clawed around his cock.

An innocent girl with no past with men was now all encapsulated in this strange surreal ride with this handsome alien. He could make her come by just looking at her, but this was beyond looking, beyond normal sex.

Even when Epsilon touched Moon, she could feel the blood thrumming loud in her veins by his mere touch. She always felt a plethora of emotions and some she couldn't recognize. She couldn't just realize that Epsilon was madly and hopelessly in love with her. He kept his rock shell around him and didn't let her know his unexpressed emotions. The only time she felt a glint of them was when he stretched her pussy with his thick cock, stretched her skin apart and pounded deep in her, and touching the base of her soul, her entirety, her center with the tip of his throbbing cock.

"I'm going to come in your pretty human pussy and make you pregnant."

He wanted to discover her, to maneuver her, to reach every nook of her body with his tongue, his fingers, and his dick and merge her soul with his own, and make their child of their dreams. Their child who would rule the world. When he would push harder inside her Moon would feel that by some strange force her body became so full and he already impregnated her a million times by planting his seeds all inside her body.

"Spread your legs as much as you can," says Epsilon between his heavy breaths.

He wasn't getting enough of this female. She just made him lost in her body and sometimes he feared that he would drown in her big mesmerizing eyes and her large sexy moans. He liked eliciting a response out of her when he would shove his dick inside her to the base of her skin and his balls would lovingly caress her back hole.

Why was this pleasure so unearthly? Completely grasping them both in its addiction.

Moon obliged, spreading her legs further while he was deep inside her.

"I will tie your hands and legs so you don't move, we are already 300 seconds in and we need to prolong it for 300 seconds more," says Epsilon, seriously looking in her eyes and not breaking their skin-to-skin contact.

Moon was about to come. Her body couldn't resist anymore but he distracted her.

"I will rub this gel on my cock and your pussy, it will pain you and sting you a bit but it will prolong our orgasm," says Epsilon while tying her legs wide apart to the bamboos. And handcuffing her hands together at the back of her ass, keeping her all pinned in place.

Her hands were tied strongly at the back. It made Moon's breasts pop out and some loose hair fall on her beautiful bosom.

Epsilon looked at her once all stretched out and wide open for him with his cock inside her. He wanted to keep looking at her but he averted his gaze pushing her hair at the back of her nape tying them too in a rope. She looked like a beautiful mermaid with hair all piled in a bun on top of her head. Now Epsilon wanted to grab her breasts tight in his both hands and fuck her for more time in an attempt to orgasm together.

Moon was looking at her mate with awe and delight succumbing to his advances.

"Ahhhhh," she moans while coming out of her reverie when she felt a stingy feeling entering inside her body.

Epsilon squirted a gel on her clitoris and labia and now it had entered all inside her.

"Keep your eyes open and keep looking in my eyes," says Epsilon, fully dazed by her beauty and now slowly rocking her, tearing her gentle skin on her vagina with his thick cock, and holding both breasts in his hands. Rubbing them and adoring them.

"You need to come with your eyes open," he commanded her. Moon looked away.

How could she not obey him?

"Fucking. Look. At. Me," Epsilon growled each word.

"And I will spank you twenty times if you disobey again," he warns her now while picking up his pace.

It was too much intensity to bear for Moon and how could she handle it and not feel it with open eyes?

The ropes were straining her feet as he fucked her, each thrust tugging on the ropes. She was secretly rubbing her quivering back hole with the back of her fingers. She knew that this will be the most powerful orgasm and her body will rip into thousand pieces as she already was outstretched for her alien. Rubbing her soft asshole while taking his full cock inside her was so hot. She arched her back to take full pleasure and length of his cock inside her while flexing her hips in low rhythms and now sliding her full finger in her ass.

"Arghhhhh..."

Moon grunted and wanted to get free out of the bounds and sit in her man's lap to fully get smitten by his hard lovemaking. But she could only move an inch and her legs would stretch apart more, making more room for Epsilon's mammoth cock.

They both felt like two people completely insatiable which prolonged their sex for eternity making them swing each other's bodies and souls. Epsilon was fully integrated into sex but he kept gazing at the 600 seconds sand timer. He had restrained for so long and in this time he could come million times inside his voluptuous human but the crude gel and gazing hard in eyes did the trick at keeping the buildup down. They would one moment revel in the sensations of his cock inside her. The other instant they would get lost in the deep oceans of their eyes, not closing for a moment so they don't ejaculate and the last grain of sand dropped in the ageold-timer. Epsilon jerked one last movement inside her pinching her eyes to close now with his lips and squawking so loud that the Cupid also shied away from this epically painful hot romance...

Epsilon sprawled on top of Moon for hours or they may have fainted for some time in their loud coming that they forgot that they successfully hatched their Miracle child. The child whose birth was to rule many generations to come. It was a calling to come, and the end of their explosion was just the beginning of a constant change in the life of Moon and Epsilon. Her breasts hugged and rubbed tightly on his hairy chest and he felt a sense of calm, and serenity run through his body lightly stroking and punching his soul. He wanted to stay inside her forever, and now his seed would stick to her womb and will come out of her sweet vagina to become a tall strong alien man, a miracle child, more handsome, and a complete warrior like himself.

A smile danced on Moon's lips while her clitoris lovingly rubbed on his pubic hair and made her quiver with a sensation. She feared coming again while his dick was still inside her and his breaths making him move and rub her clitoris, lightly pleasuring and tickling her.

Moon absorbed the sensations not daring to move her big man away from her while her finger was still inside her back hole... This man made her so hungry and she slowly pushed another finger in her ass, gently twisting them inside and reveling in the aftermath of her powerful orgasm. She felt like a goddess sweeping the man off his senses and spreading her legs fully for him.

A submissive feminine Goddess.

Nothing could kill their longing for each other. And it was interesting to see Epsilon doting Moon while their baby was in her womb because he couldn't live a day without entering her deep sweet heaven.

Their sex is his undoing to another exotic realm of pleasure.....A pleasure only slightly discovered, yet fully to be discovered and

66

cherished.....

Epsilon looked at the timer, and discovered what they accomplished. He untied Moon and held her tight in his arms.

"We did it," he said, "and I love you, little human."

"I know. I love you too."

EPILOGUE

"In a world where nothing exists, love will prevail."

Epsilon held their baby close to his chest, swaddled in cotton. He rocked the baby in his arms, watching his eyes slowly close. Once the baby was asleep, he laid him down in the bassinet, then gave the baby a kiss on his forehead.

Moon knew what this meant, now that the baby was asleep. It was time for them to unite as one.

"Get on the bed and open your legs," Epsilon commanded. Moon did what she was told, silently and obediently. He licked her wet folds up and down, grazing her clit. He lapped up all her juices. Moon was mewling under his licks. But he began to wonder,

"If you taste this good between your legs..." Epsilon thinks to himself.

"I want to drink your milk," he says while kissing her, stunning Moon with his phrase. He was a lion awakened out of his den; hungry for her milk and all her wet liquids pouring from every inch of her body.

"Do humans also crave women's milk?" thinks Moon while trying to match his dance of the tongue he played so passionately on her nipples.

"Don't move," commands Epsilon while turning his attention to suck her milk from her long-hardened nipples. He felt some white juice filling his mouth. His son drank the same milk too. The milk of this beautiful woman; while he still fucked her.

The thoughts harden his cock even more and he quickly retrieves his cock from inside her for a moment to gain his equilibrium.

Once he gained his bearings, Epsilon drove Moon into the mattress, with every thrust.

"Be a good girl and come on my cock," he commanded. Moon watched his thick hard cock plunge into her sex. His corded abs flexed and clenched with every thrust. Although she had never been with any man except Epsilon, he was the sexiest man she had ever seen.

"Yes," Moon moaned. She closed her eyes, while her sex started to clench. She could feel her release building, and she burned with desire.

"You're so fucking warm and wet."

Moon's pussy was warm and wet, soaking her mate's cock.

"Open your eyes and look at me," Epsilon rasped. Moon always felt like he could gaze into her soul, when he peered into her eyes with such longing.

"That's it, your cunt feels so good. So wet, and so tight."

His own pleasure mixed with hers, as her pussy clenched around his cock, while screaming his name. In return, he emptied hot ropes of come into her hungry, thirsty cunt.

Epsilon collapsed, pulling Moon onto his chest, and they drifted to sleep. Wrapped in his arms, Moon had never felt so safe, loved and cared for. She knew that she was *his*, always and forever.

In this world where nothing existed, this human was Epsilon's everything. His first love, the mother of his child, and his whole world. He couldn't imagine a life without Moon, and without his baby.

Moon slept deeply, and woke later when Epsilon roused her from a deep sleep. He handed her a small, tiny, and crying bundle.

"I'm sorry, he wants his mother."

Moon was already shirtless, and latched her crying baby on her breast. Once he was finished feeding, she handed him back to Epsilon. He enjoyed rocking the baby. Seeing this gentle, tender side of her alien-mate, melted her heart. She didn't know what her future held, but it didn't matter. She was happy in the present, in the now, with her alien mate.

THE END

THE WARRIOR PRINCE

Palaxian Protectors Of Earth

Book One

PREVIEW

CHAPTER ONE

RAGNAR

Knock, knock, knock.

I t was 0300 hours when I woke up from a deep sleep. I was up late, drinking my favorite occasional drink, Palaxian whiskey. I don't want to be bothered right now.

I hear knocking at my door. A voice was talking loudly from the other side of my bedroom door aboard the spacecraft I command.

"Sir, your comm device has been beeping like crazy and the main bridge communications as well. You left your comm on the bridge again."

Cadet Zark was on duty attending the bridge that night. My mind swirls in a haze.

"Cadet Zark, go back to bed. I'll call whoever it is back tomorrow."

"Sir, it's important." Cadet Zark replied.

"If Jacx calls about the part for his ship again, Brok isn't finished modifying it yet. And if you wake me up again, tomorrow you can scrub my toilet with your toothbrush," I barked back, putting a pillow over my head to silence his voice. Zark is a young Palaxian cadet. He's here to finish his pilot training. He's the same species as me. Sometimes, I think he's over-enthusiastic. He's taken on the responsibilities of my first in command, which is on medical leave.

"Sir, it's the intergalactic council. They said it's urgent." Zark pleaded.

"*Glurk*. I'll be right there," I let out a Palaxian curse.

The sound of my boots clanged against the gunmetal steel of the ship's floor. The sound echoed off the sleek metal walls and down the quiet hallway as I headed to the bridge of my craft. It's one of many Earths surveillance ships that are posted around the atmosphere to keep intruders out. The only other sounds were the comforting sounds of the ship's various equipment—the soft rumbling of the engine. The low beeps were coming from the lab. There was an urgent call from the intergalactic council that couldn't wait. That's not good. What could be so important at this hour? I left my communication device known as a 'comm' on the bridge. I cursed to myself silently for forgetting the device again as I made my way there.

I wear a t-shirt and sweatpants. A far cry from my grey, clean, pressed uniform that I usually wear. When I command my men, I want to look professional and severe. I know Jacx always looks more relaxed in his appearance when he commands his surveillance ship.

I approached the bridge and ran my fingers through my hair, trying to flatten my hair around my horns, attempting to look presentable before accepting the video call on the deck.

I sat down in my chair and pressed a button on the control panel. A holographic screen materialized in front of me.

"Ragnar, we've been calling you for 20 certations! We had to send your cadet to wake you up!"

I looked at three species of aliens staring back at me. They are a few members of the intergalactic council. The top of the council's elder is named Ronoke. I don't see him present.

"I apologize for my unkempt appearance at this hour. I didn't have time to change. My cadet informed me it was urgent. "

"Earth is under attack." Z'nar, a purple alien, replied. He's short and wide with white hair and bumpy skin.

"How could this happen?" I suddenly stood up and clenched my fists.

Another council member named Lokey, who was green with horns and a long white beard, replied.

"It's not a large-scale attack. You know Z'nar can be dramatic. One or two ships have snuck past the sky border and landed a ship there. You are the closest to the location. It seems less likely to be a violent attack, and more likely they are sneaking in quietly to steal something. And hoping to go unnoticed." Bak, the green alien, is tall and slender.

"Although we can speculate, they are armed and dangerous. We can't rule out an attack." Z'nar, the council member, replied.

"Do you know who landed a ship?" I asked.

"Zackels. That lot of reptilian species aren't exactly known for kindness." Bak, the green councilman, retorted.

"Bloodsucking thieves is the term you are looking for. They'll steal anything to sell for a few credits. Someone likely sent them," I retorted. The Zackels weren't known for their intelligence. They commonly do dirty work for others. I thought to myself.

"They don't have a reputation for anything good. They know Earth is a protected zone. Entering Earth's airspace and especially landing there breaks several intergalactic laws. Illegal planetary entry is a serious crime. What could they possibly want on Earth that they can't get somewhere else? It's a risky move just to steal something. Unless it's valuable." I questioned no one in particular.

"That's what you'll go and find out. You need to go now. There is one human on the premises. The building holds some human technology. All of which you know is extremely primitive. From what we can tell, they have landed but haven't exited their ship yet." Bak said.

"As we all know, human objects and artifacts can sell for exuberantly high prices at auction. It's become quite a problem. Peddling thieves sneaking onto Earth and stealing." Z'nar pointed out.

"This is a troublesome trend that is becoming more frequent and needs to be remedied," Bak said. "Here is the human that's in the building," Z'nar told me, as a picture of the human suddenly popped up on the giant holographic screen, switching from the elders.

"Now, here is a picture of the building she's in." It showed a white domed building.

"The location is called 'Hawaii.' We will send you the exact coordinates," Lokey, the third councilman, explained.

The picture of the human I was staring at on the large screen stirred something in me I had never felt before. An urge to protect. A desire to comfort her. I suddenly imagined myself running my fingers through her dark hair and whispering in her ear that everything would be ok. I suddenly tried to shake off the odd fantasy. By doing so, my blood boiled that this tiny human female was alone, with no way to protect herself from the Zackels. A surge of fear followed me. It was like a punch in the gut that took my breath away. If the Zackels find her, they'll kidnap her and sell her at a slave auction. Or worse, an illegal pleasure planet. There are legal pleasure planets in the galaxy. The high-class brothels don't hold their female's captive.

A species that's never before set foot onto another planet would catch a high price. The illegal brothels would do anything to get their filthy paws or tentacles on her.

After a fluctuation of emotions, I felt sick. Nauseous if I were honest with myself. I would be damned if those disgusting slimy reptiles would ever lay a googly eye, let alone a claw or tentacle, touch her. My screen flashed back to the three elders. Z'nar, Bak, and Lokey.

"Put her picture back on the screen!" My voice echoed like a boom on the bridge. I had to see her again to remember what she looked like. She had brown shoulder-length hair. Small succulent lips that seemed to seduce me innocently. Hazel eyes with eyebrows that seemed to sit on her face in a perfect spot. Delicate, but high cheekbones. She had brown skin, so unlike mine, which is blue. Her brown skin looked like smooth silk. Her brown skin was beautiful, a significant contrast from my dark blue skin.

I would love to rub my fingertips across her face, along with the tip of something else. I can see humans also don't have horns like Palaxians, such as myself. I wondered what it would be like to rub my hands through her hair without our females' small horns protruding from her scalp. I looked at her smile, no fangs either. Humans were so different from Palaxian females. The picture of the female was only a headshot. This human was beautiful. She looks like a delicate creature. My mind drifted in fantasy for a moment, wondering what below the shoulders looked like. My mind lost in thought wandered back to her slim yet succulent lips and them wrapped around my-

"Commander Ragnar? Are you alright? If you're not up to the task, we'll send Jacx, commander of the next closest ship."

"I know which ship he commands. No!" I growled. In anger, I slammed my fists down on the metal armrests of the chair. My growl and slamming fists boomed across the deck. The elders staring at me from the screen all jumped. I didn't mean to startle them.

The screen switched back to the picture of the building.

"Again, here is where she is located. You leave now. We don't know how they managed to slip past this many surveillance ships around Earth. They slipped right past you and Jacx. That's a conversation for another time." Lokey stated.

"What's her name?" I had to know.

"Brittany Kekoa."

CHAPTER TWO

BRITTANY

L ook at this picture, June," I told my best friend. I've been watching these UFOs for a while. I watch them from the telescope I modified at the Mauna Kea observatory in Hawaii. Everyone who used to work here basically left to work on space shuttle programs years ago. That industry is booming. I can still get government funding—all of which I spent modifying the telescope. Let's say it can see far. Fucking far, as a matter of fact. "Are you going on about this UFO stuff *again?"* June asks. "I've seen this ship before. And this one too." I try to convince her. She thinks I'm crazy, spending too much time alone in the observatory. I'm the last person at the observatory. Everyone has left, even the janitor, to pursue better and bigger jobs. They mostly went to work on Nasa and other private space programs. Who needs a small observatory when you can send people and rockets into space? I suppose a telescope hardly compares to massive missiles and space shuttles and space stations. Why look at space when you can send big impressive rockets there? I guess watching and observing has gone out of style. It's mostly considered obsolete. Or maybe it's those guys with a small penis complex. Trying to make up for what they don't have, I joke to myself. A lot of those rockets look like phallic symbols to me.

As I've worked alone for the past few years, I was able to improve the viewing ability of the telescope. Correction, *my* telescope. That bitch can see almost as far as the Hubble. And I've mostly kept my findings and improvements to myself, except for my best friend June. I don't think publishing the technology I've improved on to see so far and what I've seen would make me look like a credible scientist. I'd be labelled a crackpot for my UFO photographs and videos and or accused of photoshopping images just to sell them for a few bucks. So, I just publish what I call 'average Joe' work to avoid losing my funding.

"I don't think those are spaceships or UFOs," June says, eyeing the pictures I'm showing her on my cell phone. "It's probably space junk. You know, stuff that falls off of satellites and space shuttles. You know they are constantly blasting stuff into space. It's probably lost GPS satellites that broke apart or something," June says. I laugh out loud.

"Ok. You're cute, but no," I say, trying to reason with her.

"Then how do these two ship-looking objects meet in the same location? And more than once? I'm all for the space junk theory except, it would randomly float through space. These *things* don't. They leave and come back. And sometimes to the same place, like a meeting spot."

What I'm showing June is only the tip of the iceberg. I've got hundreds if not more pictures and videos of UFOs. It's not space anomalies. Or whatever it is that people call it these days. For June, it's called 'space junk.'

"It might be space junk," she says. "It is hardly space junk." I retorted. "It's more like the greatest scientific discovery ever made!"

"It's cool, whatever it is. So, what are you going to do with all this anyway? I know you've kept it a secret. Uncle Sam won't be happy if they find out that's what their tax dollars have been spent on. UFO watching," June says with a chuckle. When she puts it that way, it does sound funny; I laugh too. We've had this conversation before. It's best to keep the government out of it. They would confiscate my telescope and data. They would hire someone to photoshop all UFOs out of the images and then publish them, just like NASA. Since these findings aren't fit for the scientific community, maybe I could sell some to the Tabloids? I'll do it anonymously. I think I deserve a few extra bucks.

Well, I've called the Tabloids several times. I'll try it one more time.

Ring, ring, ring. I have my phone pressed against my ear in anticipation. I'm very anxious.

"Thank you for calling the Tabloids. This is Brandon speaking; how can I help you today."

"Hi, my name is Brittany Kekoa. I had called about selling some great UFO pictures. I sent a sample, and no one called me back."

"Oh, Miss Kekoa. It was on my plan to call back, and I apologize for the delay. Upper management decided it was best not to go ahead with this content."

"What? Why?" I ask, shocked. I thought they were kings at stuff like this.

"Well, while many people believe the Tabloids are a fake news network, we work hard to publish true things like celebrity divorces, for example. We'll feature the less popular spouse's story. So, they get a chance to explain what happened. Or when a celebrity gets wrongfully accused of a crime. And no one will listen to their side of the story. See where I'm going with this? Hoaxes we just don't do."

"This is hardly a hoax! It's real. I took the pictures myself. You can see a shadowy figure in a spacecraft through the window. You can see the shape of the windshield!" I'm distraught now. I'll defend my work, even to this jerk magazine.

"Either you are good at photoshop or a great photographer. Maybe try to contact the bigfoot hunters? Good luck to you." CLICK.

That bastard compared my work to bigfoot and hung up on me. See, this is why I was reluctant to do something like this. People have been exposed to so much fake news. They can't see the truth when it's in front of them.

It's not dark yet. I'm here at the observatory. I make way for the breakroom and grab a water bottle from the fridge. I'm way to upset to eat. I have a small camping cot to take naps on in the breakroom. I've been staying here a lot. I'll usually nap for a couple of hours before an all-nighter on the telescope. As I lay here angry, I calm down a little. I'm so close to getting more explicit images on my telescope. I need more funding. I can't get it without a good reason. They want to know exactly how it's spent. I've done pretty good fudging paperwork so far. Just one more part I need. Then I'll be able to see the faces behind the windshields of these spaceships. Right now, there's too much glare. I need an anti-glare photo lens. A big fucking photo lens, at that. I need it made in a specific way which means custom. Custom parts are expensive.

BANG. What was that?

I awake from a deep sleep.

It's dark.

I must have drifted off into a deep sleep and was more tired than I thought. It sounds like someone kicked the door down. I'm getting robbed. This can't be good. I have a desk in here also. Lucky for me, the front of the desk faces the door. I'll hide behind the desk.

When I sit at my desk, I usually leave the door open because I can see my telescope from here through the doorway. I jump off the cot and under the desk. I'm suddenly kicking myself for not getting something in here to defend myself. Seeing as I'm alone here, soon, word would get out. I've meant to get pepper spray or a taser. And now, here are lowlife thugs trying to find something to sell to pawn shops. I've got news for these idiots. The few things small enough for them to carry out of here to sell, they wouldn't even know what it is or how to use it. The only thing in here they could steal is my laptop. And I'm under the desk. I curse myself for not finding a better hiding spot. The only other place to hide in here is the bathroom. Thieves always look for desks because that's where the expensive stuff is. I tuck my necklace into my shirt. It might just look like a butterfly. It's a jump drive. Every day I backup all my photos on it. In case something like this happens. I just never thought I would be here when it did. I hear footsteps. I hear some weird voices.

Like clicks and static, it is even screeching. It's incredibly eerie. It sounds like something out of a movie. I pinch myself to see if I'm dreaming. Nope. The door to the break room opens. My curiosity gets the best of me as I hear stomping around the room. When I hear the fridge open, I peek around the corner.

OK. Did I accidentally consume a hallucinogenic? I must be tripping. I ate pizza with mushrooms for lunch. Somebody put the wrong mushrooms on my pizza.

I see a huge dark green reptilian tail. Scales included. It's coming out the back of some tight-fitting suit. It doesn't even wear shoes. It has enormous reptilian paws with huge claws. No wonder I hear all this banging around. Those claws and tail tap on the floor when he takes a step closer to bend down and dig around in my fridge.

Suddenly I feel like the kids in Jurassic Park who were hiding from velociraptors in the kitchen. Do the kids get eaten? I can't remember what happened after that.

Listen here, tappy toes, don't touch my coffee, is all I think to myself. It stands up after digging around. Then I see the nasty hand; it's scaley green like the tail and feet. I only see the back of the head, which surprisingly has green hair, of course. In his hand, I see my Starbucks cold coffee in the glass bottle. The asshole has some

84

nerve. Do lizards even like coffee? He unscrews the cap and takes a drink. Then I saw its face for the first time. It's surprisingly human-ish except for the big bulging eyes and slits for a nose, green-skin and full of nasty scales. It walks out. I correct myself; *it's* not human. It's a bipedal alien. Holy shit. Aliens are real. Except they don't look like the cute green cartoons.

I'm glad it didn't come and look under the desk. I'm not tripping; the walls and floors aren't breathing. I knew aliens were real. I suddenly wonder what they are looking for. I suddenly hear those lizard things screeching at each other. They sound mad, and I can tell they are fighting. I peek around the desk again to see what's going on. I can't believe it. They are fighting over who gets a turn to look through the telescope. Is that what they came to do? Do they know how far this can see? These two things look like toddlers fighting over a toy.

I know reptiles don't have large brains, at least here on Earth. While they are busy shoving each other off to take turns looking in the telescope, I go to the bathroom quietly. I let the yellow mellow and run back to my desk hiding spot. I hear a third one come in. Speaking in their clicking and unusually screechy and static-sounding language, I know he's scolding these two. He must be in charge. He's screaming at them. They both get quiet. He stomps around quietly. I get the feeling he's brighter than these two. I hear him opening drawers, slowly stomping around, and methodically looking through things. I listen to cabinets open and shut. More stomping around. My heart starts to race faster as I hear him come closer. I don't know how well reptiles can hear or smell. I hope he can't smell my fear or hear my heart about to burst out of my chest. Those other two aliens didn't scare me as bad as this guy. I had wondered if a trail of M&Ms would distract those other two and give me a chance to escape.

It's so quiet you could hear a pin drop. I suddenly wonder if he knows I'm here hiding somewhere. Then I hear it speaking in a scratchy click garbled voice. "Ssss Sky watcher." He said slowly, long, and drawn out. I'm suddenly terrified. He repeats it. "Ssss sky watcher. Where do you hide?" This alien knows I'm here. They know what I've been doing. I'm beyond terrified. He's come for me. I shake in fear. I suddenly hear a commotion and look around the desk again. I see more of these scaly jerks walk in. This isn't good.

I wonder if they've come to kill me. Actually, they've come to kill me. Why else would they be here? There's no way out. I can't run past them out the door. Police officers aren't coming to help. I would have called the cops already, but my phone isn't even in this room. The dispatchers would probably assume I'm crazy if I called for help. "Hello 911, lizard aliens broke in." It wouldn't go over well. Suddenly I hear gunfire, and a body hit the floor. More aliens, I wonder?

I look around the corner. I see a clean-cut military guy. Thank God help is here. As he's shooting the lizards, more rush into the building. That's a badass big gun he has. It shoots something like an electrical ball. When he misses, it doesn't blast holes in my walls. Cool. It's some secret military weapon. However, I don't know much about guns. The only type of gun I can identify is a Super Soaker. The lizard leader isn't among the fallen; he must have booked it and left his guys behind to fight. Well, you know what they say about being a snake. The big military guy is looking around. I don't pop out from under the desk just yet. I don't know if he's a friend or foe. He could have come for me, just the same as those aliens.

The military guy called someone. I hear his deep voice calmly say. "The area is clear of the Zackels, but I have not located the female." So that's what the lizardmen were called. Zackels. I make a mental note. As for me, I'm just 'the female.' I'm just not sure about this guy, so I stay hidden. Although my mind is slightly out of sorts, something about him seems a little off. I can't pinpoint just what exactly. I'll stick with my gut instinct; it's not been wrong yet. As the military man comes into the break room, my makeshift bedroom for all-nighters, I suddenly hear more gunfire. I guess he was wrong about the area being alien free. I hear more of them come in.

"There is more oncoming." He speaks.

He shoots his gun and is looking for cover. I see him come this way. He's shooting and walking backward. Those Zackels are shooting towards me now. I quit peeking and hide under the desk again. He walks behind the desk and gets down on one knee. He's behind the desk, directly behind me now. He shoots some more of those scaly bastards from over the top of the desk. I hear them hit the floor. I'm under the desk as far as I can go with my head pressed to the floor. I have my hands clasped on the back of my head. I'm not dead yet. I'll hold on for dear life even if I only have my head to hold on to. I hear a few more shots, and then he stops shooting. I can't see him with my head ducked down, although I listen to him say, "There were more Zackels on the premises. The area has now been cleared. I did not locate the female, only one male." This guy, the nerve of him. I've got news for this guy; I'm not a male.

What an exciting accent. I wonder where he's from? He has a deep but raspy voice. I lift my head slightly up and turn around, poke him hard in the chest, and say, "I'm over here, big boy." Wow. His chest is hard. Why am I thinking about that right now? I poke it again, just to satisfy my curiosity. Since I might be blasted to bits, I let my mind wander. It's been a while since I've had a man. He gets down on all fours, crouched down like me now, looking me in the eye. But he lifts one hand and runs it through my hair, speaking in a language I don't understand. I smack his hand, and he pulls it back. "I don't speak that language, English big boy. Keep your hands off me," I say—what a jerk. I feel so violated. Who does he think he is? Does he think he can touch me like that? I don't even know his name.

"Your hair. You cut it. Very short. Comparable to a male standard cut, "he says.

"So, instead of planning our escape, you want to talk about fashionable haircuts?" The nerve of this guy! I don't know why my feelings are hurt that he might not dig my new cut. He responds with a few grunts.

"Listen here, Encino man, I don't like your tone. And for your information, Hawaii can get very hot in the summer. I don't need all that hair in the heat. The air conditioning here doesn't work very well anymore. So, it was a practical thing to do." I snap back. I don't know why I am compelled to explain myself defensively.

"Practical." He says back, sounding more like a question. He's staring into my eyes silently. I feel like he's judging me, and I don't know why I care so much. I notice his dark blue eyes, which are bright at the same time. They look like the midnight sky. As I look into his blue eyes, why do I feel as if something here is off? I can't pinpoint exactly what. When all was said and done, at least he apologized. "I'm sorry," he says sympathetically.

www.ingramcontent.com/pod-product-compliance
Lightning Source LLC
Chambersburg PA
CBHW071546150726
48000CB00002B/963